The Magic School Bus®
A SCIENCE CHAPTER BOOK

POLAR BEAR
PATROL

SCHOLASTIC INC.
New York   Toronto   London   Auckland   Sydney
Mexico City   New Delhi   Hong Kong   Buenos Aires

Written by Judith Stamper.

Illustrations by Steve Haefele.

Based on *The Magic School Bus* books
written by Joanna Cole and illustrated by Bruce Degen.

The author would like to thank Don Moore, PhD,
of the Central Park Wildlife Center
for his expert advice in preparing this manuscript.

ISBN 0-439-31433-X

24 23 22 21 20 19 18   7 8/0

Designed by Peter Koblish

Printed in the U.S.A.   40

INTRODUCTION

Hi, my name is Tim. I am one of the kids in Ms. Frizzle's class.

Maybe you've heard of Ms. Frizzle. (Sometimes we just call her the Friz.) She is a terrific teacher, but a little strange. One of her favorite subjects is science, and she knows everything about it.

The Friz takes us on lots of field trips in the Magic School Bus. Believe me, it's not called *magic* for nothing! Once you step on that bus, anything can happen!

Ms. Frizzle likes to surprise us, but we can usually tell when she is planning a special lesson — we just look at what she's wearing.

One day Ms. Frizzle came to school in an ice-blue dress covered with bears. But these weren't cute little teddy bears. Oh, no. They were big white polar bears — the kind that live near the North Pole.

Right away, I knew we were in for an adventure — one that would take us to the top of the world!

CHAPTER 1

"Brrr-r-r-r, it's freezing in this classroom," Phoebe said with a shiver. "It feels like the North Pole!"

I was shivering, too. But I thought it was just my imagination. I was looking at pictures of the Arctic on the Internet. The Arctic is a region that includes the icy Arctic Ocean and the regions surrounding it. Our class was studying Arctic animals, and I needed facts about polar bear babies — fast!

"Phoebe, if you're cold, you can use my blubber experiment," Ralphie offered. He was doing a project about blubber. It's what keeps lots of Arctic animals warm.

"Ms. Frizzle," Dorothy Ann said, "I think I know why it's so cold. Somebody turned on the air conditioner. And I'll bet I know who did it!"

Our eyes followed D.A.'s gaze across the room to Arnold. He had pushed his desk close to the air conditioner. On top of the desk was his igloo project. Ice cubes were melting all over his desk.

"But I had to do something," Arnold said. "My project was turning into a puddle!"

"Well, that explains why we don't live in igloos around here," the Friz said. She walked over to the air conditioner and shut it off. "Of course, building an igloo is a good way for people to stay warm if they live in the Arctic."

"How do I make an igloo that won't melt? I guess it's back to the drawing board for me," Arnold sighed.

"How do all those Arctic animals stay warm without igloos?" Wanda asked.

"According to my research," Dorothy Ann said, "most Arctic animals have adapted to the freezing weather."

"Like growing blubber under their

skin," Ralphie said. "That's how seals stay warm."

"Or having thick fur and living underground," Carlos said. "That's how lemmings stay warm."

Keeping Cozy in the Arctic
by Dorothy Ann

How Arctic Animals Stay Warm

Seals have a thick layer of blubber.

Musk oxen have a two-layered coat of fur.

Lemmings have furry bodies and build tunnels underground.

Polar bears have a layer of blubber and thick, hollow hair that helps hold in their bodies' heat.

"Watch out, I'm coming through," Arnold said. "My igloo has turned into slush!"

Arnold picked up his project and dumped it into the sink.

"Don't worry, Arnold," Ms. Frizzle said. "You'll figure it out by tomorrow."

Tomorrow! That was when our Arctic projects had to be done. My project was on the polar bear. And my research was going great — except for one little problem. I couldn't find facts about polar bear babies.

"Ms. Frizzle," Keesha said. "I think there's an animal missing in the Polar Baby Parade."

Uh-oh! It was my animal that was missing. No Polar Baby Parade would be complete without a baby polar bear!

Ms. Frizzle walked over to Keesha. She was staring at a wall of the classroom that was covered with pictures of baby animals that lived in the Arctic. They were lined up in a cute little parade. Each animal had facts about it written underneath its picture.

"Let me see," Ms. Frizzle said, checking out the animals. "Here's a baby Arctic fox . . .

and a young musk ox . . . and a little caribou . . . and a teeny lemming . . . and a baby seal. . . ."
All of a sudden she stopped
walking along the parade of baby
animals.

"Hmmm, it's Tim's animal
that's missing," the Friz said. She
gave me a surprised look. "But
don't worry, Keesha. I'm sure
that everyone will get their project
done on time."

I groaned. I could *barely* believe my
baby polar bear was missing. I always like to
be the first one done with a project.

I walked over to Ms. Frizzle and whispered in a low voice so Keesha couldn't hear.
"Ms. Frizzle, the books in the library didn't
have a thing about polar bear babies," I said.

From the Desk of Ms. Frizzle

What's in a Name?

The word *polar* comes from the word *pole*. The polar bear got its name because it lives near the North Pole.

"I checked out every one," I explained. "Now I'm trying to find information on the Internet."

I had found lots of cool facts about polar bears, but nothing about babies.

"Well, someone had better hurry up," Keesha said. "Or one baby is going to miss the parade."

I sighed under my breath and stared at the computer screen. My baby wasn't going to miss the parade. The polar bear was King of the North. I'd make sure the polar bear baby was at the head of the parade!

Just then, I found what I was looking for — the website of the Polar Bear Research Station. I clicked on the picture of a mother polar bear with two cubs.

And did I luck out!

"Ms. Frizzle, a scientist at the Polar Bear Research Station has an on-line chat right now. Can I ask him a question?" I asked.

The Friz leaned over my shoulder to check out the website. She saw the scientist's name — Luke Iglulik. A big grin spread over her face.

"Go right ahead, Tim," she said.

I typed in my first question:
What time of year do polar bear babies come out of their dens?

Seconds later, I got an answer:
In the spring, about four or five months after they are born.

I typed in my second question:
How many babies does a mother have at one time?

The answer came right back:
A polar bear mother has from one to four babies. Usually there are two bears in a litter.

Then Ms. Frizzle leaned over my shoulder and typed in a message:
Hi, Luke, remember me? Valerie Frizzle.

I couldn't believe it! Ms. Frizzle even knew a scientist in the Arctic!

A message came right back:
Do I remember you? How could I forget? You always drove that yellow motorcycle in college. I hear you drive a wild school bus now. Why don't you come up for a visit?

Ms. Frizzle chuckled. "Tim," she said, "would you like to find out about polar bear babies in person?"
"Wow," I said. "How cool would that be!"
"Very cool, Tim," the Friz said. "Like fifty degrees below zero!"

Ms. Frizzle typed in a message:
We're on our way, Luke. See you there, bear!

Luke wrote back:
Will do, caribou!

Ms. Frizzle didn't waste a minute. She jumped up and ran to the supply closet. A few minutes later, she came out — in the strangest outfit ever!

The Friz had on a blue parka and pants covered with polar bears!

Cool Clothes for the Cold
by Keesha

The first parkas were made of pieces of reindeer skin sewn together. The reindeer hide was worn on the outside. The soft fur was worn on the inside for warmth.

A parka has a hood because lots of body heat is lost through the head!

CHAPTER 2

"Ms. Frizzle," Arnold asked nervously, "what's going on?"

"How about a sleepover in a real igloo, Arnold?" the Friz asked.

"I don't think so," Arnold said. "I promise not to turn on the air conditioner again!"

Now everybody was crowded around the Friz.

"Why are you dressed in a snowsuit, Ms. Frizzle?" Phoebe asked. "It's April."

"Because we're going on a trip," the Friz said. "Your snowsuits are already on the bus."

"But . . . but . . ." Arnold stammered.

"Hurry up, everyone," Ms. Frizzle

11

called. "We're headed for the Arctic! Just follow me."

We ran out to the parking lot. The Magic School Bus was sitting there. It had a big sign on its side: ARCTIC EXPLORER.

I grabbed a seat in the front of the bus beside Dorothy Ann.

"Fasten your seat belts, kids," Ms. Frizzle instructed. "The Arctic Explorer is ready for takeoff."

The Friz started the engine of the Magic School Bus. We cruised out of the parking lot onto the road. Soon, the sound of the bus turned into the roar of jet engines. I looked out the window. The Magic School Bus had sprouted wings!

WHOOSH! We were up in the air!

Arnold peered out the window.

"Bye, Mom. Bye, Dad," he said. "It's been nice knowing you."

"Arnold," I said, turning around. "You don't have to worry. Ms. Frizzle is behind the wheel."

"That's exactly what I *am* worried

about," Arnold said. "And I don't like the look of those polar bears on her parka."

"Polar bears don't usually eat humans, Arnold," I said. "As long as people stay out of their way, that is."

"Well, that seems like a good reason not to get in their way!" Dorothy Ann said.

King of the Arctic
by Tim

Polar bears are at the top of the Arctic food chain. They mostly eat seals. Polar bears do not attack humans unless provoked.

"Where are we headed, Ms. Frizzle?" Carlos asked.

"To the Polar Bear Research Station in Alaska," the Friz answered. "It's just inside the Arctic Circle."

Ms. Frizzle pressed a button on the control panel. A little movie screen popped down over our heads. It showed a map of the Arctic.

"Do you see the North Pole?" Ms. Frizzle asked. "It's at the very top of the world and in the middle of the area that is called the Arctic Circle."

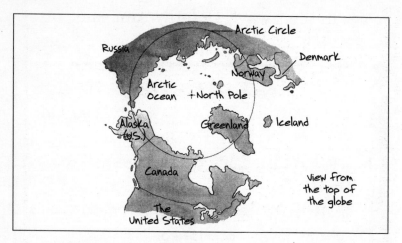

"What's the Arctic Circle, Ms. Frizzle?" Keesha asked. "And who drew it?"

"The Arctic Circle is an invisible line, Keesha," the Friz answered. "It marks the region at the top of the globe — the most northern part of the earth."

"And it's where you can find polar bears," I said excitedly.

Polar Bear Country
by Tim

   Polar bears live all over the Arctic polar region. Five nations can call themselves part of the polar bear country.

- The United States
   (Polar bears only live in the state of Alaska.)
- Canada
- Russia
- Denmark
   (Polar bears live on the island of Greenland, which is part of Denmark.)
- Norway

The Arctic Explorer wasn't wasting any time! Down below us were miles and miles of forest. We were covering ground fast.

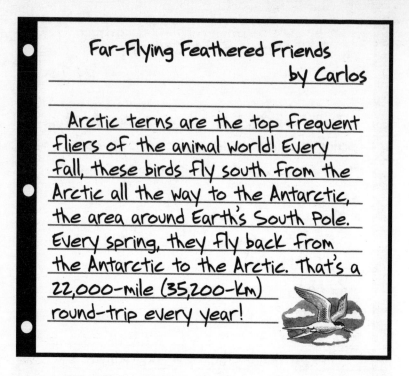

Far-Flying Feathered Friends
by Carlos

Arctic terns are the top frequent fliers of the animal world! Every fall, these birds fly south from the Arctic all the way to the Antarctic, the area around Earth's South Pole. Every spring, they fly back from the Antarctic to the Arctic. That's a 22,000-mile (35,200-km) round-trip every year!

"Hold on, kids," the Friz announced. "I'm dropping in altitude. There's something down there you've got to see."

A few seconds later, the plane dropped down like a roller coaster. All of a sudden my ears popped and my stomach was left somewhere on the ceiling.

"This had better be good," I moaned.

The Friz turned around with a twinkle

in her eyes. "It's going to be tundras of fun, Tim," she said.

We all craned our heads to look out the windows. Down below us was something really cool. The green blanket of trees covering the ground suddenly stopped. Beyond it stretched the low Arctic tundra, a treeless, marshy land.

"It's the tree line!" D.A. shouted. "I read about that."

The Tree Line
by Dorothy Ann

The tree line is where trees no longer grow and the flat tundra begins. Why do trees stop growing along this line? Because the ground north of the tree line is frozen all year-round. The frozen ground stops large tree roots from taking hold. Mostly mosses, herbs, and small shrubs grow in the tundra regions.

"Hey," Carlos said. "I thought the Arctic was covered by mountains of snow and ice."

"Don't worry, Carlos," the Friz said. "There's plenty of snow and ice ahead. But right now we're flying over the tundra. In winter, it's covered with ice, too. Now that it's spring, the snow is starting to melt."

"I think we've gone far enough, Ms. Frizzle," Arnold said. "Why don't we just make a quick visit to the tundra? We can observe a little melting snow — and then head home."

"Forget about the moss," I said. "I want to see some baby polar bears."

"And I want to see a baby caribou," Keesha said. "Baby caribou are so cute. They've got to be the cutest polar babies around."

"I'll bet baby polar bears are cuter," I said.

But just then, everything around us turned icy! The plane started to bounce up and down. We were flying in the middle of an Arctic snowstorm!

"I knew I should have stayed home today," Arnold kept saying over and over.

Well, it was too late now! I looked out the window. I couldn't see a thing. The air was solid white.

"Hold on tight, kids," the Friz shouted. "I'm making an emergency landing."

The plane dropped down, down, down. It hit the ground with a bump. Then it slid along the ground like an out-of-control sled. Finally, we skidded to a stop.

For a few minutes, we just sat there in

shock! We couldn't see a thing outside the windows. The air was filled with snow.

But we could hear something. And it sounded weird — like a broken car horn. Finally, D.A. broke the nervous silence. "Ms. Frizzle, what's that scary noise?"

"I'm not sure, Dorothy Ann," the Friz said. "You kids should put on some more warm clothes. Then we'll investigate."

Our overhead compartments popped open. And down fell parkas, snow pants, boots, and gloves.

We all dived for the clothes. It took a while to put on all the layers. Arctic explorers have to dress in layers.

"Follow me," the Friz said. She opened the door to the plane, and a slide popped out to the ground. One by one, we zoomed out onto the ground.

Just then, the blizzard stopped. The strange noises got louder. And we could see where it was coming from.

"Reindeer!" Wanda yelled.

"Those aren't reindeer," Keesha corrected her. "They're called caribou, and they're close relatives of reindeer."

We had landed in the middle of a huge herd of caribou! The strange noise was them bleating.

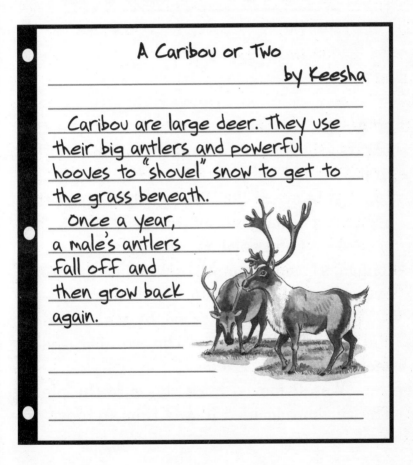

A Caribou or Two
by Keesha

Caribou are large deer. They use their big antlers and powerful hooves to "shovel" snow to get to the grass beneath.

Once a year, a male's antlers fall off and then grow back again.

CHAPTER 3

The caribou were nibbling at the tiny plants growing on the tundra. Keesha was the first to spot a baby.

"A baby caribou!" she gushed. "Isn't that the cutest thing you've ever seen?"

The baby caribou was standing on its long legs beside its mother. When its big brown eyes saw Keesha, it let out a bleat.

"Be careful not to frighten them, Keesha," the Friz warned. "They're not used to seeing people."

We all moved back closer to the plane. The caribou decided it was time to move on.

Caribou Calves Learn Fast
by Keesha

A caribou calf is up on its feet when it is only one hour old! When it is only one day old, a baby caribou can run faster than a human. To survive, caribou calves have to be able to escape from predators – fast!

We watched as the whole herd headed farther north. Keesha waved good-bye to the baby.

"I wish I could have petted the baby," Keesha said.

"It's better if we don't interfere," Ms. Frizzle said. "It's usually not good for people to disturb wild animals."

"I guess I wouldn't like it if a caribou barged into my bedroom, especially if it didn't knock," Carlos remarked.

"What will we do now?" Phoebe asked.

From Ms. Frizzle's Arctic Notebook

Caribou and Oil Don't Mix

There is a huge area of protected land in Alaska called the Arctic National Wildlife Refuge. Many environmental groups are worried that drilling for oil in the refuge will be harmful to the Arctic animals that live there. One of the places drilling might be done is very close to where caribou have their calves each spring.

"The only way I'll get back in that plane is if it is headed home," Arnold insisted.

"You don't have to get back in the plane, Arnold," the Friz said. "Turn around."

We turned around to look at the Arctic Explorer. But it wasn't a jet anymore! It had turned into a gigantic snowmobile.

"All aboard!" Ms. Frizzle shouted. "We've got to get going. That storm slowed us down. We still have a lot of ground — I mean, tundra — to cover."

We jumped into the snowmobile behind Ms. Frizzle. She started the motor. And we shot off across the snow.

"Next stop, polar bears!" I yelled.

CHAPTER 4

The Magic Snowmobile was huge! It had runners like skis on the bottom. And with the Friz at the wheel, we were truckin' across a sheet of thick ice.

I couldn't wait to get to the Polar Bear Research Station. I wondered if I would see real polar bears there. With the help of Dr. Luke Iglulik, I would do the best Arctic project of all!

"Ms. Frizzle," Ralphie yelled out. "Can you please put on the brakes?!" I looked at Ralphie. He was pointing at something ahead of us. It was a brown spot on the ice. Ms. Frizzle slowed the Magic Snowmobile to a stop.

"What's up, Ralphie?" the Friz asked.

"Look over there," Ralphie said with excitement. "It's my Arctic animal!"

Sure enough, Ralphie had spotted a seal.

"Good thing I brought my camera," Ralphie said. "I'll have pictures to go with my blubber experiment." He pulled a camera out of his pocket and snapped away.

"I see the seal," Wanda said. "But where's the blubber?"

"It's under their skin," Ralphie explained. "The blubber keeps them warm, like insulation."

Blubber Underwear
by Ralphie

Blubber is a thick layer of fat right under the skin. Blubber keeps in body heat and keeps out the cold. For a seal, it's like wearing woolly underwear!

"I want some blubber," Arnold said with a shiver.

Very quietly, we climbed out of the Magic Snowmobile and walked toward the seal. But as we came closer the seal slid down the hill to the other side.

"All right, class," Ms. Frizzle said, pointing to the hill of ice in front of us. "Let's climb up and check out where we are. Maybe we can see the seal on the other side."

I made it to the top of the hill first.

"Wow!" I said to myself.

"Wow what?" Ms. Frizzle said, coming up behind me.

"Wowee!" I whispered.

In front of me stretched the Arctic Ocean. Big chunks of pack ice floated by. It seemed to go on forever.

Ms. Frizzle and the rest of the kids scrambled up beside me.

"There's the seal!" said Ralphie in an excited voice. "And a baby!" He snapped some quick pictures.

"Arctic seals usually live by themselves,

but a mother takes care of her baby until it is ready to take on the world," Ms. Frizzle said.

Seal Pups
by Ralphie

A mother seal gives birth to just one seal pup at a time. The pup stays in a snow-covered den. A seal pup in its den is easy prey for a polar bear. The seal's chances of survival are better when it goes out on its own. And even though polar bears are great hunters, a seal often gets away.

We were quietly watching the mother seal with her baby from the top of the ridge.

Then, suddenly, something strange happened. The seals seemed to get nervous. Even the little pup was anxious. And they didn't hang around for much longer.

Plop. Plop. The seals hit the water. We could see another seal family in the distance. All those seals dived into the water, too.

"I wonder what happened," Dorothy Ann said. "I don't think they saw us up here."

"Maybe they saw — or sensed — something else, like an enemy," I guessed. "Maybe there's a polar bear around!"

That made everybody shiver and look around.

"I wanted more pictures of the seals," Ralphie said, "for my project."

"No problem, Ralphie," Ms. Frizzle said. "Head back to the Magic Snowmobile."

We slid down the ice hill and jumped back into the snowmobile.

Ms. Frizzle started the engine and took off. All of a sudden I realized she was going backward!

"No!" I screamed as we headed for the

water. "You're going the wrong way!"

The Friz just smiled at me. Oh, no, I thought. Her brain has frozen!

Everybody was yelling at the top of their lungs. But the Friz stayed right on course. We were backing into the ocean! But just as we got to the edge of the ice, something strange happened.

The Magic Snowmobile changed shape. It closed up all around us. We hit the water with a splash.

"Welcome to the Magic Sub," Ms. Frizzle said with a grin.

I breathed a sigh of relief. The water outside the windows looked really cold!

"Seals!" Ralphie yelled. He whipped out his camera again. A family of seals passed by us. They waved their flippers for the camera.

I was happy for Ralphie. He had gotten to see seals. And I guess I was even happy for Keesha. She had seen a whole herd of caribou. But we were invited to the Arctic for my project. And I hadn't seen one polar bear yet!

Ms. Frizzle came out of the sub's galley.

She was carrying a tray of food.

"Who wants a sub sandwich?" she asked. "It's the house special!"

We all dived in. Then we took our subs to eat by the porthole windows. We didn't get this view in the normal school cafeteria!

We settled down to eating our subs. The seals seemed to be happy drifting along beside us. But suddenly, they all darted away.

"Look, Tim," Dorothy Ann said. "What's that white thing by your porthole?"

I looked out and saw what looked like a huge paw zoom by. I almost jumped out of my seat. Could it be what I hoped it was?

"Whoa. That fish looked an awful lot like a bear," Phoebe said.

"It *was* a bear, Phoebe," I said proudly. "And he sure can swim."

The Polar Bear Paddle
by Tim

Why are polar bears such great swimmers? Here are the facts:

- Polar bears have big forepaws that are partly webbed to help them swim.
- Polar bears use their back feet like a boat rudder to guide them through the water.
- Polar bears can see food underwater from up to 15 feet (4.6 m) away!
- A polar bear's fat layer keeps it warm in cold water and helps it float.

The bear was swimming so fast that we couldn't see him very well. I could just make out his back legs. His fur was all wet and streaming behind him.

"Please follow that bear," I called out to Ms. Frizzle.

The Friz turned the sub around to follow the bear. All of a sudden, the bear headed for the surface. We watched it pull the back end of its huge body up out of the water.

"Hurry up," I said. "Let's go after it!"

"I think we should wait awhile," Ms. Frizzle said. "We don't want to follow the bear too closely. Besides, maybe we'll see something interesting from down here."

The Friz was right, as usual!

We hovered in the water close to where the polar bear crawled out of the ocean. A few minutes later, a seal swam past us. It went up to the surface to take a breath of air through the hole in the ice.

That was its last breath of air ever! We saw a big white paw break through the water.

It knocked the seal on the head. Then the seal was pulled up out of the water like a fish.

Blubber-licious
by Ralphie

Ninety percent of a polar bear's diet is made up of seals. And a polar bear's favorite part of the seal is the thick layer of blubber under its skin.

When a polar bear kills a seal, it usually eats only the skin and blubber. The blubber provides the bear with both energy and water. The skin provides vitamins.

A polar bear usually catches only one seal every four to five days. But then it has a feast. An adult polar bear can eat up to 150 pounds (68.2 kg) of blubber for one blubber-licious meal!

"GROSS!" Phoebe said. "That bear is mean."

"It's not mean," I said. "That's how the bear stays alive."

"Let's go up someplace else," the Friz said. "We should let the bear eat in peace."

The Magic School Sub chugged along under the ice. Then the Friz said, "Prepare for surfacing."

The Magic School Sub popped up out of the water. Ms. Frizzle steered it up to the ice. Then she pressed a button and two treads came out of the bottom of the sub. With their traction-action, we revved up onto the ice.

When Ms. Frizzle opened the hatches, I was the first one out of the sub. So I got to see them first.

"Cool!" I yelled.

They were white. They were furry. They were two polar bear cubs!

CHAPTER 5

When we popped up, guess what we saw? The best polar babies in the Arctic — polar bear cubs!

"I want to pet them," Wanda said. "But I know, I know — I can't!"

"That's for sure," I told her. "Remember, they're polar bears, not teddy bears!"

We watched the cubs play. Then they took a break to clean their fur.

One of the cubs hit the other with its paw. Soon, both cubs were rolling in the snow.

From Ms. Frizzle's Arctic Notebook

White, but Not White

A polar bear's fur looks white. But it is really colorless. Polar bears look white because their hair scatters and reflects light — just like snow does.

Polar bears clean themselves up after a messy meal of seal. They roll in the snow or take a dip in the freezing water.

"How old do you think they are, Ms. Frizzle?" I asked.

"They're still little," Ms. Frizzle said. "That means they were just born this winter."

"Where do you think their mother is?" Arnold asked nervously.

"Probably hunting for food," Ms. Frizzle said. "The cubs are still too young to help out."

It's Not Easy Being Green
by Carlos

Three polar bears in the San Diego Zoo once turned green. Green algae was growing in the hollow center of their hair. Scientists at the zoo cleaned up the algae and made the bears white again!

Everyone watched the cubs play — until Arnold turned around, that is.

"Uh, everybody," Arnold said. "Company is coming."

"Don't be silly, Arnold," Wanda said. "We're out in the middle of nowhere."

"I think you'd better look," Arnold said.

"Oh, all right," Wanda answered.

We all turned and looked across a narrow strip of water. About 50 yards (46 m) away, we saw the polar bear that had passed us underwater. The bear was staring at the polar bear cubs. Then she turned her eyes on us and let out a growl.

"Yikes! It's the mother bear!" Ralphie shouted.

Suddenly, the middle of nowhere got really loud. The mother polar bear let out another, louder growl. The cubs started squealing. And we all screamed!

The mother polar bear dropped the bloody seal she was carrying. Then she reared up on her back legs. Another growl shook the air.

Big Bears!

by Tim

An adult female polar bear weighs from 330 to 660 pounds (150 to 300 kg). An adult male is even bigger! A male weighs from 650 to more than 1,600 pounds (295.5 to 727.3 kg).

From Ms. Frizzle's Arctic Notebook

Polar Babies

A polar bear mother digs a den in the snow to have her babies in November. The babies are born about six weeks later. At birth, a baby cub weighs less than 2 pounds (0.9 kg)! They are blind, deaf, and helpless in every way.

The mother feeds the babies milk, and after 10 weeks the cubs weigh about 20 to 25 pounds (9.1 to 11.4 kg). In March, they leave the den with their mother to go out into the Arctic spring.

"Ms. Frizzle, think of something!" I said. "She thinks we might hurt her babies!"

"Back away from the cubs," Ms. Frizzle ordered. "Maybe she'll calm down."

But the mother bear didn't look calm. She looked really, really angry. She started across the ice toward the water that separated us.

"What will we do?" Arnold whimpered. "I don't like bear hugs!"

I saw a dead fish on the ice and picked it up. "Maybe I can throw this at her," I said. "Maybe she'll stop to eat it."

But it looked like nothing was going to stop the mother bear. She charged across the ice and then dove into the water.

Dive Right In!
by Wanda

A polar bear can dive from the top of an iceberg 50 feet (15.2 m) into the water!

Arctic Athletes

by Tim

Polar bears are strong and fast! They can run as fast as 35 miles (56 km) an hour for a short distance. Polar bears have been known to swim more than 60 miles (96 km) without a rest!

"How fast do polar bears swim?" Arnold asked me nervously.

"Fast," I said. "But not as fast as they can run!"

"Ms. Frizzle, please save us!" Arnold yelled.

We all turned around, ready to run. And did we ever get a surprise!

The Friz had done it again! The Magic Sub was gone. In its place was an Arctic dogsled pulled by 12 husky dogs. Behind the main sled was a smaller supply sled.

I looked closer at the lead dog's face. It looked a little strange. In fact, its eyes reminded me of the Magic School Bus's headlights! Right away, I decided we should call the dog Bright Eyes.

"All aboard, kids," the Friz called out.

As I ran for the sled, I tossed away the fish I had found. I noticed that it fell into the supply sled, but there was no time to get it out. I jumped into the big sled with everyone else.

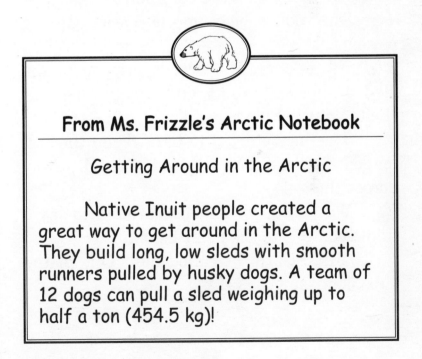

From Ms. Frizzle's Arctic Notebook

Getting Around in the Arctic

Native Inuit people created a great way to get around in the Arctic. They build long, low sleds with smooth runners pulled by husky dogs. A team of 12 dogs can pull a sled weighing up to half a ton (454.5 kg)!

"Ms. Frizzle," Arnold screamed, "she's coming!"

We looked toward the water. The mother polar bear had swum across the water between us and was pulling herself onto the ice. She was only about 50 feet (15.2 m) away now! The bear stopped to shake out her fur.

"Everyone's in. You can step on the gas, Ms. Frizzle!" Dorothy Ann said nervously.

"There is no gas," the Friz said. She was frantically checking the dogs' harnesses.

The polar bear mother was getting closer.

All at once, Ms. Frizzle jumped in the sled, grabbed the reins, and cried, "Mush!" at the top of her lungs.

The dogs started to bark. Then they all leaped forward. We started to pull away across the ice.

We'd escaped! I turned around to say a final good-bye to the polar bear cubs.

"Ms. Frizzle," I called out. "One of the cubs is missing."

"Don't worry, Tim," the Friz said. "Its mother will find it. We're out of here!"

"Mush!" we all yelled.

I wasn't sure what "mush" meant. But it sure worked. Bright Eyes and the rest of the dogs took off like lightning. Soon, we were flying across the snow and ice.

The polar bear mother was slowing down now that she was satisfied that we could no longer harm her cubs.

Man's Other Best Friend
by Arnold

Not all Arctic peoples use huskies to pull their sleds. The Lapp people ride in sleds pulled by reindeer!

CHAPTER 6

There is nothing that can compare with riding in a dogsled. That is, unless you get the chance to *drive* a dogsled!

"Tim," Ms. Frizzle called. "Can you take over the reins for a while? I need to check my map."

My knees were shaking as I moved to the front of the dogsled. Ms. Frizzle handed me the heavy leather reins.

"What if I have to stop the sled?" I asked nervously.

"I'm not sure," the Friz said with a frown. "What is the opposite of mush?"

I took the reins and hoped we wouldn't have to stop! The dogsled flew across the ice.

"Look," D.A. yelled. "An Arctic fox . . . and its babies! I think they're my favorite."

Ralphie snapped a picture.

A Foxy Fox
by Phoebe

The Arctic fox changes its fur coat twice a year. In the winter, its fur is white and thick. The white fur blends in with the white snow to protect the fox from enemies. In the summer, the fox sheds the white hair to show a thinner coat of brownish-gray fur. That coat matches the tundra landscape after the snow has melted.

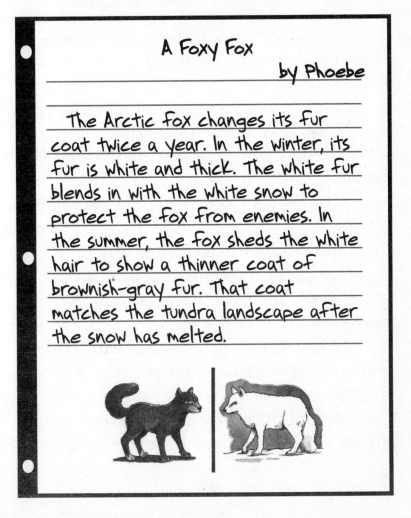

Beside me, Ms. Frizzle pulled out her map. "We're heading in the right direction, Tim," she said. "Do you want to stay behind the wheel — I mean, reins?"

Did I ever!

"Mush!" I yelled.

The lead husky turned around and flashed its eyes at me. Bright Eyes sure was loving this ride!

An hour later, my arms were getting really tired from holding the reins.

"When will we get there?" I asked Ms. Frizzle.

"I'm tired," I heard Phoebe say. "What time is it?"

Ms. Frizzle looked at her watch. "Leaping lemmings, it's eight o'clock at night!"

"But it can't be," Ralphie said. "Look at where the sun is in the sky."

"Even though it's getting late the sun won't set for a little while yet," the Friz explained.

"According to my research, the sun is out for about 14 hours in April, so it'll set soon," D.A. explained. "It's a good thing we didn't take this trip four months ago when it was dark for almost the entire day."

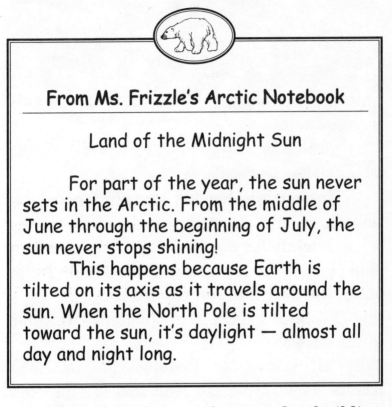

From Ms. Frizzle's Arctic Notebook

Land of the Midnight Sun

For part of the year, the sun never sets in the Arctic. From the middle of June through the beginning of July, the sun never stops shining!

This happens because Earth is tilted on its axis as it travels around the sun. When the North Pole is tilted toward the sun, it's daylight — almost all day and night long.

Just then, I saw a low wooden building in the distance.

"There it is," Ms. Frizzle said. "The Polar Bear Research Station."

The huskies headed straight for the station. As we got closer, I pulled tighter on the reins. Luckily for me, it worked. We came to a stop right in front of the station. A man burst out of the door and ran toward us.

"Valerie Frizzle," he shouted. "Welcome to the Arctic!"

"Hi, Luke," Ms. Frizzle said. "Dr. Luke Iglulik, meet my class. And this is Tim. He's doing the research on polar bears."

"Hi, Tim," Dr. Luke said. "Let me help you with the dogs. They must be tired and hungry after a long journey."

From the Desk of Dr. Luke

Huggable Huskies

Husky dogs usually work in teams of 11 or 12. The one or two dogs that run in front are lead dogs. They set the pace for the others.

Each dog needs to eat 2 pounds (0.9 kg) of good food a day. Most people give their huskies names and enjoy their personalities. You can't beat having a husky for a best friend in the Arctic.

"I'm tired and hungry, too," Arnold said.

"In the North, we always take care of the dogs first," Dr. Luke explained. "You might need them to save your life."

We unhitched the huskies from the sled and fed them. Then we started to unpack our supplies.

The Friz pulled back the canvas tarp on top of the little supply sled at the back.

Did we get a surprise! Curled up there was a white ball of fur. It was one of the polar bear cubs!

"Uh-oh," Arnold said. "His mother is going to be really, really mad at us!"

"Did you take this cub away from his mother?" Dr. Luke said. He sounded really upset.

"Not on purpose," I said. "He must have crawled into the supply sled."

"He probably smelled this," Dr. Luke said, holding up the skeleton of the fish I had picked up.

I felt terrible! The cub was miles away from his mother. And it was all my fault!

"Is he old enough to live without his mother?" I asked Dr. Luke.

"We can keep him safe for a while," Dr. Luke said. "But he needs a mother to teach him how to survive in the Arctic."

"Let me help you take care of him," I

I hope the cub can *bear* with us till we find his mom.
If the mom doesn't find us first.

said. "I want to know everything about polar bear cubs."

"We'll put him in a pen inside the research center tonight," Dr. Luke said. "Tomorrow we'll try to find his mom."

Dr. Luke picked up the white ball of fur and carried him into the research station. He put the cub in one of the pens there.

Ten minutes later, I was helping feed the cub from a bottle. I started to feel a lot better.

"What are you feeding him?" Phoebe asked. I could tell she wanted to help. So I let her hold the bottle for a while.

"It's as close to his mother's milk as possible," Dr. Luke explained.

Power Milk

by Tim

A mother polar bear feeds her cubs milk until they are about two years old. Polar bear milk is so rich that it is more than 30 percent fat!

Soon, the little cub curled up in a ball and fell asleep. I started to yawn, too.

"It's time you had some dinner and hit the sack," Dr. Luke said. "Come on into my igloo."

"Igloo!" Arnold yelled. "I know all about those. I can't believe you live in an igloo."

"Actually, igloo is the Inuit word for any house," Dr. Luke explained. "*Igluvigak* is the term for a snow house. My ancestors were Inuit. Some people call us Eskimos, but we call ourselves Inuit."

Arnold led the way out of the research station and into Dr. Luke's igloo. We crawled through the low entrance into a big room.

We all settled down on the rugs on the floor of the igloo.

"I like to carry on the old ways as much as possible," Dr. Luke explained. "I made this igloo the same way that Inuit did a century ago."

A pot was cooking over a little stove. Dr. Luke served each of us a bowl of soup. While we ate, he told us how the Inuit used to hunt polar bears.

From the Desk of Dr. Luke

To build an igloo all you need is a snow knife and tundra snow.

1. Mark a circle in the snow. Cut out the first blocks from the center of the circle. Make the blocks about 2 feet (61 cm) wide and half a foot (15.2 cm) thick. Lay each block on its edge on the ground around the circle. Shave off the tops of the blocks so that they slope down and slant in.

2. Lay the next row of blocks, tilting them in a bit to narrow the circle. Spiral more rows of blocks upward and inward.

3. Place the last block, or keystone, on the top. Fit it from the inside. Fill the joints between the blocks with snow.

4. Cut a low tunnel near the bottom of the house. Add more snow blocks to create an entrance. [4]

"For my ancestors," Dr. Luke said, "life was very hard. To make it through the long winter, they had to hunt animals to survive."

"But wasn't it dangerous to hunt a polar bear?" I asked.

"Yes, very dangerous," Dr. Luke said. "An Inuit hunter would track a bear's footprints in the snow. When the bear was in sight, the hunter would let loose his dogs to attack the bear. While the dogs surrounded the bear, the hunter would throw a harpoon at the bear to kill it.

"My ancestors called life 'a long walk on an empty stomach,'" Dr. Luke said. "They had great respect for the polar bear. They called it Nanook."

From the Desk of Dr. Luke

Nanook, the Great White Bear

The polar bear was the most dangerous animal to hunt. And it was greatly respected for its strength and spirit.

The bear's blubber, meat, and fur all helped the Inuit survive. And the Inuit gave thanks and respect to Nanook. After a hunt, they held a celebration that lasted for days. Then, a polar bear dance was held. Finally, the bear's skull was set on an ice floe to release its spirit back into the Arctic.

CHAPTER 7

That night, I dreamed I was in a refrigerator — and it needed to be defrosted! I thought my dream had come true when I woke up stiff and cold. But then I saw Arnold sleeping beside me . . . and it all came back. We were having a sleepover in an igloo!

As soon as I smelled breakfast cooking, I scrambled out of my sleeping bag. Dr. Luke was cooking oatmeal over a stove. Ms. Frizzle was adding dried apples and raisins to the pot. I helped make hot chocolate. By the time everyone was awake, breakfast was ready.

"You kids are in luck that I had enough

oatmeal. I usually have fish for breakfast," Dr. Luke said.

Fish for breakfast? Oatmeal never tasted so good.

After we finished breakfast, Dr. Luke asked me to go with him to check on the polar bear cub. We crawled out of the igloo and walked to the research station.

"How old do you think the cub is?" I asked.

"Polar bears give birth between November and February," Dr. Luke said. "It's April now . . . so I'd guess the cub is about four to six months old."

When we went inside the research station, the cub was cuddled up in a ball in its pen.

"Come on, little fella," Dr. Luke said. "We're going to take you back to your mother."

"But how will we ever find her?" I asked. "The street signs aren't so great around here."

"Valerie, I mean Ms. Frizzle, thinks she can retrace your tracks from yesterday," Dr. Luke explained. "Today, we'll start back to where the cub hitched a ride with you. The mother will probably stay in that area to search for her baby."

We fed the cub again so he wouldn't get hungry during the ride. A short time later, we packed up the dogsled. Bright Eyes was in the lead again. He licked my hand and flashed his eyes on and off as if he couldn't wait to get going.

Luke stowed the bear cub in the supply sled again. We all climbed into the big sled.

"Mush!" everyone yelled.

The sled took off, heading back to the cub's home territory. We flew across the smooth ice with Bright Eyes providing the dog-power.

A short time later, the sled climbed up an ice ridge. On the other side was an amazing sight!

"Hey, have we traveled back in time?" Carlos asked. "Those things look like woolly mammoths!"

"I know what they are," Wanda said with excitement. "They're my favorite Arctic animal — musk oxen."

The Magnificent Musk Ox
by Wanda

Musk oxen are big, shaggy animals that roam the tundra. They travel in herds of females and their young led by one or two strong males. The males fight over who will be leader by butting their thick heads and horns against each other.

The musk ox's long, curved horns keep away enemies. When a herd smells nearby wolves, all the musk oxen form a circle and face out. They lower their heads to show off their horns. The wolves trot away — to wait for a sneak attack.

"They have a double layer of hair that keeps them warm. And, look, there's a baby!"

The musk ox calf was cute — for a musk ox. But it couldn't compare to my polar bear cub.

"Anybody hungry?" Ms. Frizzle called out.

"What's for lunch?" Arnold asked.

We soon found out. Try to imagine what really, really cold peanut-butter-and-jelly sandwiches taste like. Let me tell you, they take a long time to chew!

While we ate, we stopped the sled close to the edge of the water so we could watch for whales.

We spotted a killer whale and a walrus. These two huge Arctic animals are the only creatures a polar bear steers clear of.

"Time to pack up, kids," Ms. Frizzle said. "We've got a long trip ahead of us."

I looked across the water. Two young polar bears were on the icy shore. They were having a play-fight. It looked like a professional wrestling match!

Arctic Giants

by Tim

The polar bear is the King of the Arctic. But two other animals can cause it trouble. One is the walrus, which can weigh up to 2,200 pounds (1,000 kg). The walrus has 3-foot (91.4-cm) tusks that Keep a polar bear from messing with it. Polar bears and walruses have been Known to attack and Kill each other.

Another Arctic giant is the black-and-white Killer whale, also Known as an orca. Polar bears eat dead whales that have washed ashore. But live Killer whales may attack a swimming polar bear.

I heard a whimper behind me. The polar bear cub was watching the males fight. He looked afraid. And I knew why. Male polar bears will kill cubs that get in their way.

We really needed to get the little guy back to the safety of his mother!

Polar Bear Punches
by Ralphie

Young polar bears wrestle in the snow to build their strength and skills. They practice using their strong paws, and they show off their big, sharp teeth.

As adults, male bears fight with each other over a female. Each male fluffs out his coat of fur to make himself look bigger. Then he swaggers along, growling, to scare off his rival. Polar bear scientists call this "the cowboy walk."

Dr. Luke picked up the reins and started to turn the sled around.

"Uh-oh!" we heard him say.

And soon we knew why! While we were eating, the ice beneath us had broken away from the mainland. We were floating in the Arctic Ocean. On a piece of pack ice!

"Now what do we do?" Arnold asked.

"Look around," Ms. Frizzle said. "This may be the only chance you get to hitch a free ride in the Arctic Ocean!"

"I hope so," Arnold mumbled.

Go With the Flow!
by Arnold

In the spring and summer, Arctic ice breaks up to create ice floes. Ice floes are huge pieces of ice that break off and float in the Arctic Sea. Polar bears often hop a ride on an ice floe to get to a new hunting ground.

"Tim, look over to the left," Dr. Luke called out. "Those polar bears are saying hello." I looked over and saw two bears walking around each other.

Polar Bear Pleasantries
by Phoebe

When two polar bears meet, they have a special way of greeting each other. They circle around each other for a while, grunting. Then they come closer and touch noses.

We floated along for another hour. Then Ralphie let out a yell. "We're going to crash!"

Seconds later, we crashed! Right into land. Our ice floe ground to a halt.

Ms. Frizzle checked her Global Positioning System—a device that can pinpoint your location using satellites. "Luke, we've landed close to where we found the cub," she said. "That ice floe saved us some time!"

"Let's get the sled over the top of this ridge," Luke said. "Then we can start looking for the cub's mother."

Bright Eyes and the team really had to pull to get the sled over the ridge. When we were done, Luke said we should take a break to give the dogs a rest.

"Ms. Frizzle, everybody," Keesha yelled, "the weirdest thing is happening over here!"

We all turned to see what Keesha was talking about. She was pointing at a line of tiny brown animals that were running across the ice. D.A. told us they were lemmings. There were hundreds of them. No, thousands!

"Wow, what's going on?" I asked. "Where are they going in such a hurry?"

"They have no idea where they're going," Dr. Luke said. "They're just following their instincts. It's one of the weirdest things in the animal world."

"That gives you something to think about," Ms. Frizzle said. "Don't always follow the crowd."

Leaping Lemmings!

by Carlos

Lemmings are fat, furry plant eaters that live in burrows. They multiply very fast. In just one month, a female can have up to 10 baby lemmings. About five weeks later, those lemmings are having babies.

Every three or four years, lemmings run out of food and space – especially if they live on a peninsula or in another small area. Many leave to find a new home. Soon, millions of lemmings decide to follow the crowd. A huge mass of lemmings run across the tundra. Foxes and owls kill many of them. Many others blindly rush along. They fall off cliffs. They drown in the ocean.

The lemmings that are left have enough food and space to survive.

I decided to check on the polar bear cub. While everyone was watching the lemming parade, I walked away to have a look at him.

But when I got to the supply sled, I was in for a surprise. I lifted up the supply shed cover, and the polar bear cub was gone!

CHAPTER 8

I started to yell to Dr. Luke about the missing cub. But he was busy telling the other kids more about the lemmings. I decided to search for the cub myself. After all, it was my polar baby project.

"Bright Eyes, want to come with me?" I asked the lead husky.

Bright Eyes jumped up, ready to go. I unhitched him from the reins. Then we climbed up the ice ridge together.

"How far away could a little cub like that get?" I asked out loud.

Bright Eyes just barked and ran ahead. We reached the top of the ridge. I looked out over the snow that stretched toward the water. I saw a little ball of fur running across the ice. It was the cub, and he was heading for the water.

"Hey, stop!" I yelled. But the cub just ran on. His feet were like snowshoes on the ice.

Furry Footwear
by Wanda

A polar bear's feet are nature's perfect snowshoes. The bottoms are wide and covered with fur to make them nonslip. The sharp claws help grip the ice.

I ran down the ridge after the cub. Then, *boom,* my feet slipped out from under me and my bottom hit the ice.

"Whoaaa!" I yelled.

I zipped down the slope like I was on a superfast sled. I could hear Bright Eyes barking behind me. But he couldn't keep up. I slid all the way down the slope and out onto the ice. When I finally stopped, I was right beside the polar bear cub!

The cub started to walk farther out on the ice to the water. I got up and started to follow him. Until I heard Bright Eyes bark.

I stopped and turned around.

"What's the matter, boy?" I asked. "Come with me."

But Bright Eyes let out a low growl and took two backward steps. He looked like he was trying to motion me back to the ice ridge.

"Okay, I'll get the cub myself," I said, stomping my foot on the ice.

Just then, a crack as loud as thunder echoed under my feet! I looked down. The ice was breaking up all around me!

I took a step toward the cub. Maybe I could get ahold of him and carry him back. But a big crack ripped across the ice between the cub and me.

I heard Bright Eyes bark louder. Now I was really scared. And it wasn't just for the cub. I was walking on thin ice!

I tried to take another step back. But the ice kept cracking. I didn't know what to do but freeze in my tracks. I was trapped!

"Bright Eyes," I yelled. "Go get Ms. Frizzle and Dr. Luke. Hurry!"

Bright Eyes barked and ran up the ridge.

I turned around to look at the cub. He was sitting on the ice and whimpering. I felt like whimpering, too. Then the cub got up and started to squeal. I turned around to see why.

"Yikes!" I yelled. It was the polar bear mother. She was running down the ridge toward us.

The cub kept squealing. I wanted to

squeal, too. But I was scared stiff! What if the mother bear came out onto the ice? Her weight would sink us for sure!

Of course, my worst fears came true! The big polar bear took several steps across the sheet of ice. But then she did something really amazing. She got down on her belly and started to creep toward us. She was pulling herself along with her claws. I was really freaked out, until I remembered my research. Polar bears are Arctic experts. They know how to travel on thin ice.

Polar Protection
by Tim

Mother polar bears will do anything to protect their young. They can kill a predator with just one swat of their powerful front paws. Scientists have even seen a mother polar bear stand up and leap at a helicopter to keep it away from her cubs.

From the Desk of Dr. Luke

The Ice Crawl

A polar bear can crawl across ice too thin for a human to walk on. They spread out their legs and lay their bellies flat on the ice. Then they use their claws to slowly push themselves across the ice.

The cub watched his mother. Then he got down on his belly. I didn't waste any time. I got on my belly, too.

Slowly, the mother bear turned around and headed back toward land. The cub crawled after her. I brought up the rear.

"Tim!" I heard Ms. Frizzle scream.

I looked up and saw Bright Eyes on top of the ridge with the Friz, Dr. Luke, and the other kids.

I was so happy to see them that tears came to my eyes. But they turned into icicles the minute they hit my cheeks.

Dr. Luke was running down the ice ridge. I saw that he had a rope in his hands. Ahead of me, the mother polar bear and the cub were creeping across the ice. I heard another loud crack behind me. A huge chunk of the ice broke off and flowed away into the ocean.

Dr. Luke stopped running when he got to the edge of the thin ice. He threw out the rope to me. It almost reached. Almost!

I kept crawling along the ice, pretending I was a polar bear. The rope was just out of my reach. Then it was closer. Then I grabbed it!

Dr. Luke pulled me in like a big fish. Bright Eyes licked my face with his warm tongue. I was safe!

"Th-th-th-thanks," I said through chattering teeth. "That was close."

Ms. Frizzle gave me a big hug. Then she pointed across the snow. "Look, Tim," she said. "Your cub is safe, too."

I sat up and looked across the snow. The polar bear mother was there. She was licking her cub and cuddling him. Then I saw the other cub. He came bounding down the ridge to join his family.

"Mission accomplished," Dr. Luke said. "Now we had better get you back to the research station, Tim. We don't want to take any chances with frostbite!"

From the Desk of Dr. Luke

Count Your Toes

Arctic explorers have to watch out for a frozen danger: frostbite. Frostbite strikes when skin is exposed to extreme cold. Ice crystals form in the skin and even beneath the skin. If gangrene, or tissue death, occurs, a person could end up losing fingers or toes — or even a limb.

At the time, I didn't know what frostbite was. And I'm glad I didn't!

The rest of the kids helped me up the ridge. I stopped to rest at the top and turned around to look at the cub. I saw him raise one of his paws up in the air.

I like to think he was waving good-bye.

CHAPTER 9

"Hey, everybody, I got my pictures back!" Ralphie yelled. He ran into the classroom. The rest of us were putting the finishing touches on our Arctic projects.

We all crowded around Ralphie to see. The first pictures were of Ralphie's seals.

"These go up behind my blubber experiment," Ralphie said.

"Look," Wanda said. "Here's my musk ox baby. Isn't it cute?!"

"And here are some pictures of those lemmings!" Carlos said. "I wonder where they've gotten by now."

"Hey, there's the polar bear swimming," I said, looking at the next picture. "Wow, I can't believe we were there!"

"And I'm happy we are all back — safe and sound," Ms. Frizzle said. "How are your fingers and toes feeling, Tim?"

I wiggled my fingers for everybody to see. I had been scared of frostbite for a while. But now I was feeling fine — and I loved all the attention.

"Tim, here's a picture of you with your polar bear cub," Ralphie said.

I looked at the picture. The little cub was probably snuggled up against his mother right now, taking a nap.

"Add him to the polar baby parade," Keesha said. "In the place of honor."

I took the picture and taped it to the wall — right at the head of the whole parade!

"Hey, everybody," we heard Arnold call out. "Check out my igloo."

We ran over to Arnold's desk. On top of it, he had built a perfect miniature igloo out of sugar cubes!

"It's not as big as my last one," Arnold said. "But it's not going to melt."

"I think it's sweet, Arnold," Ms. Frizzle said with a smile. "And I have a treat for the rest of you — for doing such a great job on your Arctic animal projects."

Ms. Frizzle disappeared into her supply room. Minutes later, she walked out with a tray full of special treats.

"Eskimo pies!" we all yelled.

"That's *Inuit pies* to those in the know," Carlos chimed in.

No matter what we called them, they were a tasty way to celebrate the end of a cool science unit.

Tim's Project
A Polar Bear's Life Cycle

1. A mother polar bear digs a den in the snow. She has her babies — usually two — between November and February. The babies weigh less than 2 pounds (0.9 kg) at birth. They drink their mother's milk and grow fast.

2. By March or April, the cubs weigh from 22 to 33 pounds (10 to 15 kg). They leave the den and follow their mother across the snow to the coast. They watch her hunt for seals, and they play and tumble in the snow.

3. During the first year, the cubs begin to eat solid food but still nurse from their mother. They begin to learn to hunt and swim. But they can't live on their own.

4. By the time they are two years old, the cubs have grown into large bears. They leave their mother and strike off into territory of their own. They hunt and live alone. But they play with other bears they meet.

5. Polar bears are ready to mate when they are five or six years old. They are adults by this time and weigh 330 to 660 pounds (150 to 300 kg).

6. Both male and female polar bears live to be as much as 30 years old.

Join my class on all of our
Magic School Bus adventures!